PUFFIN BOOKS

The House that Moved

'Move the old Tudor House!' Adam cried. 'How can they possibly do that?'

The City Council's decision to move the old house, in order to make way for the new relief road, caused a stir in Exeter. The house was only going to move three hundred yards down the road, but Adam and Donald couldn't imagine how it was going to be done. They had used the derelict old house for ages as their own secret place and so they were determined to be involved when the move took place. Though nobody could possibly have guessed just how involved they were going to be!

A fascinating story, based on a a real event.

David Rees was born in 1936, and went to King's College School, Wimbledon, and Queen's College, Cambridge. He taught in schools in France and London and is now a Lecturer in English at St Luke's College, Exeter. Since 1975 he has published novels for children and teenagers. His hobbies include surfing, listening to music and tracing the family tree. He is married, with two sons.

DAVID REES

The House that Moved

Illustrated by Laszlo Acs

PUFFIN BOOKS

PUFFIN BOOKS

Published by the Penguin Group
Penguin Books Ltd, 27 Wrights Lane, London W8 5TZ, England
Penguin Books USA Inc., 375 Hudson Street, New York, New York 10014, USA
Penguin Books Australia Ltd, Ringwood, Victoria, Australia
Penguin Books Canada Ltd, 10 Alcorn Avenue, Toronto, Ontario, Canada M4V 3B2
Penguin Books (NZ) Ltd, 182–190 Wairau Road, Auckland 10, New Zealand

Penguin Books Ltd, Registered Offices: Harmondsworth, Middlesex, England

First published by Hamish Hamilton Children's Books Limited 1978
Published in Puffin Books 1982
5 7 9 10 8 6

Copyright © David Rees, 1978
Illustrations copyright © Laszlo Acs, 1978
All rights reserved

Printed in England by Clays Ltd, St Ives plc
Set in VIP Plantin

For Adam

Author's note

The house that moved is a real house that stands at the bottom of West Street in Exeter. Next door to it is a ladies' hairdressing salon the owners of which are friends of mine called Barry Webb and Barry Casley. In 1962 when most of the old West Quarter of the city was being pulled down to make way for the construction of the Inner Bypass, many people thought that the Tudor house on the corner of Frog Street and Edmund Street should be preserved, although it stood directly in the line of the proposed new road. The City Council agreed, and so it was transported three hundred yards to its present site, using the machinery and methods I have described, though the whole operation took much longer than I have suggested. The house has no particular historical significance, but it is a beautiful example of the architecture of the early sixteenth century. It is now used as a jeweller's shop.

The Teignmouth Inn was demolished in exactly the way as it is in the story, but the loss of the West Quarter was not all a tale of sad destruction. Over the centuries the river had shifted its course and left the ancient Exe Bridge high and dry; houses were built over it, but, when they were pulled down, the eastern half of the bridge was revealed once more, battered, but on the whole marvellously intact. Together with the ruins of St Edmund's church it is an impressive monument, the longest medieval bridge left in England. You can walk on it and underneath it, and explore the remains of buildings even older than the Tudor house itself.

Adam and Donald liked to play in the derelict old Tudor house that stood on the corner of Edmund Street and Frog Street. It had long stood on its own because all the buildings near by had been pulled down to make way for the new relief road. They weren't supposed to play in the house for the Council now owned it; it was boarded up and a notice said NO ADMITTANCE, but there was a back door somebody had forgotten to lock. It was a very small house. There was only one room on the ground floor, from which stairs led to the only room on the first floor, but the top, which was the biggest storey and

jutted out into Frog Street, had two rooms. One of these was Donald's, and one was Adam's. Here they kept their things and played all kinds of games, and sometimes they invited special friends up for murder or hide-and-seek, or to have a picnic. It was dark and dirty in the Tudor house, but Adam and Donald didn't mind. There was even some furniture the last inhabitants had left, an old armchair, a rickety table, a mattress and some cushions.

'You won't be able to play in there much longer,' Adam's father said one day at teatime. 'They're going to move the house.'

'Move the house!' Adam cried. 'How can they possibly do that?'

'I don't know, but they're going to try. It says so in the evening paper. It's to be moved three hundred yards and joined on to our house. And the Teignmouth Inn is to be demolished.' Adam's family lived at the end of West Street; Dad was a hairdresser, and they lived over the shop. A sign hung under Adam's bedroom window: BARRY WEBB. LONDON HAIR FASHIONS.

'Whatever will they think of next?' Adam's mother said. 'Mr Cazeley bought that Tudor place for two hundred pounds, just so he could pull it down and widen the entrance into his garage! Then the Council said he couldn't. Then they bought it back from him. Now they're going to move it!'

'The paper says it will cost ten thousand pounds,' said Mr Webb.

'We have to pay for that out of our rates!' Mrs Webb exclaimed, indignantly. 'Ten thousand pounds!'

'Can I go out now, please?' Adam asked.

'Yes. But be careful in that old house. The workmen are going to start on it tomorrow.'

'Have the Council told us they're going to put it next door?' Mrs Webb asked. 'It's a bit of a nerve! Whatever will we do with our dustbins?'

'I think I had some notification,' Mr Webb answered. 'I put it away somewhere.' He didn't like official letters, particularly ones from the City Council, and he usually stuffed them into a drawer of his desk and forgot about them. 'Adam, remember what I said about being careful!' He looked round, but Adam had already gone.

Next morning, when Adam and Donald arrived at the Tudor house, they found they could not get inside. A gang of workmen was busy unloading huge pieces of timber from a lorry and stacking them against the back door. 'What are they for?' Donald asked.

'I don't know,' Adam said. He turned to one of the men, the boss he imagined; this man seemed to be supervising the others rather than helping them to lift the massive

beams off the lorry. 'Hey, mister! What's all that wood for?'

'You'd be surprised,' he answered, and walked away.

'Not much help,' Donald said, but when the man returned, he asked, 'Mister, can we go in there, please?'

'Inside the house?' He laughed. 'No, you certainly can't!'

'Our things,' Adam said. 'They're in one of the rooms.'

'What . . . you play in there, do you?' They nodded. 'Get in through the back door?' They nodded again. He looked at them sharply for a moment, then produced a bunch of keys from his pocket and unlocked the front door. 'Wait there,' he said, and went inside.

'What's he doing?' Adam wondered.

'I don't know,' Donald answered.

After a few moments the man came back

and said, 'Well, you don't seem to have done the place any harm; I'll say that for you. But you're not to tell anybody I let you in, or I'll be for it.'

They promised they wouldn't breathe a word. They had never been through the front door before; it creaked and groaned because it was so stiff from not being used.

'That's nice,' said Donald. 'I always wanted to come in that way.'

'Why?'

'Because it's our house, yours and mine, and everyone else has a front door, so why shouldn't we?'

Adam didn't really mind which entrance they used so long as they could go in and out. Donald was always fussier about details; once he had got into trouble with his mother because he had removed some spare curtains from the linen chest at home and taken them to the Tudor house. They had spent what

Adam thought was a rather dull morning trying to hang them up over a window on the top floor. Their efforts were not very successful because there was no rail or pole, and when Mrs Martin discovered her curtains were missing, they had to be taken back, and Donald was in trouble for removing them without asking.

But the Tudor house had many more uses than just being a make-believe home. It was so old that everything about it made the two boys think of the past; it stood in a quarter of Exeter that had been inhabited for nearly two thousand years. The games they played in there all had some connection with history. At times it was a Roman watch-tower on the city walls, and they were centurions on the look-out for marauding British savages who inhabited St Thomas, the district they could see across the river from the top floor. Yesterday it had been the scene of an unsuccessful attack by

Cromwell's soldiers in the Civil War; they and several other members of the Royalist garrison had poured dozens of barrels of boiling oil over the enemy who were trying to climb up the side of the house. Once it had been a hospital during the cholera epidemic and they had nursed each other back to health, even though the doctors had pronounced them dead three times; and last week it had withstood the assault of Nazi bombers on that terrible night in May 1942 when the city had been blitzed. All this local history they did not learn at school; it came from Adam's father, who loved all the old tales about Exeter, even if he paid little attention to what the present-day Council said when they wrote letters to him.

This morning, however, was not a time for games of any sort. What the workmen were doing was far too interesting, and also quite mystifying. The first job they did was to erect scaffolding all round the house, and after that they began bolting the pieces of timber to the walls, as if they were trying to encase the whole thing in some kind of box.

'When they've finished,' Adam said, 'perhaps they'll put a steel cable round it and just drag it away.'

'It would fall over,' Donald said.

'Maybe they're going to put it on wheels.'

'Stupid! How can you possibly put a house on wheels?'

'I don't know. I can't see how else you can move it.' Adam walked over to the window and looked out. One of the men on the scaffolding waved to him, and asked if he was enjoying himself. 'Yes, thank you,' he answered. He turned to Donald and said, 'I wish they'd go away. It's our house.'

'It isn't really,' Donald said, sadly. 'It was all pretend.'

Adam scowled. 'I bet you anything you like they won't let us in tomorrow.'

'We must make them.'

'How?'

They both thought for some time. The problem was to find a way of persuading the workmen that they could be useful; that was the best method of ensuring that they would not be turned out. 'We could give them cups of tea,' Donald suggested. 'They all went off at eleven o'clock for their tea-break and they were away for ages! They probably had to go to the café at the top of Fore Street.'

'That's a good idea.'

Donald brightened up; he had thought it sounded rather feeble. 'The only trouble is there's no water in here, and even if there was, there isn't a cooker. And I don't think my mum would like us boiling kettles.'

'Nor would mine. But we could *bring* them cups of tea, couldn't we? If I could get Mum to . . . Yes, why not?'

Over dinner Adam bombarded his father with questions. Mr Webb knew most of the answers, for the only topic of conversation in the salon that morning had been what was happening to the Tudor house. The mayor's wife had come in for a shampoo and set, and she was a mine of information on the subject. And she did hope Mr Webb agreed with the plans for the new road; it was so necessary to relieve all those horrid traffic jams that clogged the High Street all day long. His reply was non-committal, but with other customers he made his views somewhat clearer. It was awful that so much of the old city was being pulled down for the sake of cars, he said.

Adam listened to his father sounding off on that subject, then extracted from him everything he wanted to know about what the workmen were doing. As he had guessed, the timber was being bolted to the house to stop it collapsing when it was moved. When that part of the job was finished they were going to fix iron wheels to its four corners, then lift it up bodily on pneumatic jacks. What was a pneumatic jack, he asked. The same principle as a car jack, Mr Webb told him, only it was much more powerful and much larger; it was operated by compressed air. And there wouldn't be many difficulties lifting the house up; being so old it had no foundations. It would be gently winched out into Frog Street, and hauled very very slowly up the hill on iron rails, until it arrived next door to the shop. The journey was only three hundred yards, but it would take several hours. Workmen were coming on Friday to prepare the new site; the Tudor house would have some proper foundations at last.

'What's going to happen to it when they get it here?' Mrs Webb asked.

'Builders doing it up. Then it's being rented by an antique dealer.'

'An antique dealer!' Mrs Webb sounded disapproving. 'I don't know whether I want one of those right on our doorstep.'

'Why not?'

'They're always hand in glove with crooks,' she said, vaguely. 'Stolen candlesticks and all that.'

'You watch too much rubbish on the telly,' said Mr Webb. He stood up and wiped his mouth. 'I must go back to work; Miss Ash is waiting downstairs for re-styling. Come to think of it, we'll be on the telly ourselves. They'll surely want to film the house moving.

We can wave at the cameras out of the kitchen window.'

When his father had gone, Adam asked his mother about the workmen's tea-breaks. Much to his surprise she had no objection, provided she, and not Adam or Donald, made the tea. He would have to take it down to the Tudor house himself; she was much too busy to do that. And she could offer them biscuits, if they wanted. 'I expect they get up a good thirst in this weather,' she said. 'Nothing like a cuppa when you've a good thirst, and it's certainly turned hot today.'

The next problem was to do a deal with the boss. Donald should try this, they thought; Adam was not very good at being tactful. Anything delicate he met head on. The boss thought it was a very kind gesture; speaking for himself, and on behalf of all his men, tea three times a day at eleven, half past

one, and four, would be extremely welcome, and so would biscuits. And of course they'd pay Mrs Webb for the trouble.

'There's a snag,' Donald said. 'A condition.'

'What's that, then?'

'We'll only do it if you go on letting Adam and me play in the house.'

The man laughed, loud and long. 'That's blackmail,' he said. 'Yes. Blackmail. You'll go far, you will. Now then, let me think.' Donald watched him while he thought, feeling the battle was already won. The boss was a large fat man with a florid red face; he looked kind, the sort of person who would try hard not to refuse a child's request. 'All right,' he said. 'You win. There's only one thing. Some parts of this job, it will be dangerous inside that house, so you're certainly not staying in there then. O.K.?'

'O.K.!' Donald agreed. 'And thank you

very much!' He ran off to find Adam and tell him the good news.

And so it worked out during the next two days. It took all that time for the men to bolt the pieces of timber and the wheels to the house, to lay the iron rails, and to check that their expensive equipment was in perfect working order. Their presence, however, did not always distract the boys from their usual games.

'If the house is Tudor,' Donald said one morning, 'do you think Henry the Eighth ever stayed here?'

'No. But Katharine of Aragon spent her first night in England in Exeter. There was a colossal thunderstorm. A sort of warning to her, my dad said.'

'I wonder if it was this house.'

'It's a bit small.' Adam jumped, startled; there was a face at the window, grinning. It was one of the workmen, but for a moment he had thought it was Queen Katharine herself.

'My dad says there used to be a lodging-house for tramps in this street,' Donald said. 'They slept on the floor and made their own cocoa.'

So they played at being tramps; it was a better idea than Katharine of Aragon. 'Can you spare me some cocoa?' Adam asked.

'Yes.'

'And some sugar to go with it?'

'Get lost!' So to earn his sugar, Adam had to put in a morning's hard work breaking stones. But eventually he was promoted and made a trusty, in charge of all the other tramps to make sure they didn't come in drunk.

Then it was time, he decided, to play something in which he gave the orders instead of Donald. He was William of Orange, demanding the surrender of the city. King William had landed at Brixham, not far down the coast, and Exeter was the first town of any importance he had had to contend with in his attempt to dethrone James the Second. He had come through the West Gate, which had stood only a few yards away from where the hairdressing salon now was. Adam had often read the plaque on the wall: 'Site of West Gate. Successfully defended against the rebel attacks in 1549. William, Prince of Orange, with his army, entered the city in 1688 through this gate which was removed in 1815.'

'My Lord Governor, do you surrender this city . . . and all who sail in her?'

'Go away, you old frump!'

'Frump!' Adam tumbled backwards, laughing. 'What sort of a word is that?'

'Well . . . how can you sail in a city?'

'You can't. It just sort of came out.' He cleared his throat. 'I'll start again. Surrender this city or I'll put you to the sword!'

'We remain ever faithful to his majesty, King James!'

'Do you! Well, you've had it now!' A fight ensued, in which Donald's head got banged, accidentally but rather hard, against the wall.

'I'm tired of this,' he grumbled. 'Let's see if we can help the workmen instead.'

So they spent the next half hour passing nuts and bolts up to the men on the scaffolding. They imagined they were back in Tudor days, building the house; it was almost as good, Adam thought, as playing inside it.

At half past four on the Thursday afternoon the boss shouted up to Adam and Donald that they must come down in ten minutes' time; the move was about to start.

'Can we come back after?' Adam asked.

'After what?'

'Tomorrow, I mean.'

'Certainly not! Tomorrow's moving day proper!'

'So it's the end,' Donald said. He walked away from the window and rubbed the wall with his hands. 'I like it here. I don't want it moved. I like this wood.' He sniffed it. 'It smells of old things.'

'They'll probably let us in when it's on the new site,' Adam answered, trying to be cheerful.

'They won't. There'll be people inside repairing it and painting it. They won't want *us*. And when it's finished that antique dealer will have it.'

They wasted the last few moments being miserable. They listened to the final hammerings, the chatter of the workmen as they stood back and surveyed their achievement. The boss called up: 'Time to go!'

'Goodbye, old house,' Donald said, standing in the doorway of his room. It had always been empty and abandoned, ever since he'd first been in there, but he'd peopled it so often, furnished it in his mind. Adam said nothing. They went downstairs.

They had to duck as they came out of the front door. A great beam of oak had been fastened across it. The boss locked the door.

'You'll be here tomorrow, I expect,' he said, 'to watch the move? You'd better come early; there'll be hundreds of people.'

'Yes,' they said. And Donald added, 'Thank you for letting us play in there.'

'Ah, you were no trouble.'

They walked away, down towards the river. The whole area had been cleared; the relief road was so important. Only a few isolated buildings remained, including the Teignmouth Inn in Edmund Street. The landlord and his wife, Mr and Mrs Brealy, had gone months ago and the place was shut up; the tiles had been stripped from the roof and the inside gutted. Tomorrow Edmund Street and Frog Street would be closed to traffic by order of the police. This was so the Tudor house could be moved unhindered, and so that all the television people and the newspaper cameramen could have as easy a view of it as possible. It also meant that the demolition gang could take advantage of the closure of the streets to pull down the Teignmouth Inn. That was to be the side attraction to the main event, the house on wheels.

Adam and Donald stopped by St Edmund's church and looked back. The men already had their equipment under the house, had lifted it up a few inches. They were only going to carry out a test now, just move it off the place where it had lived for four hundred years to make sure it did not start to disintegrate. Then they would leave everything until tomorrow. Adam glanced up at the church clock, but remembered that that was no use. The clock had stopped that night, years before he was born, when Nazi bombs had rained down on the city; the church roof had been destroyed and nobody had bothered to repair it. St Edmund's wasn't considered an important monument, even though there had been a church on that spot for centuries, for much longer than the Tudor house had existed. It would probably be demolished, though a decision had not yet been made. It wasn't in the way of the new road. It was simply that no-one wanted it nowadays.

Clearing the old houses had revealed all sorts of interesting things. Part of the medieval bridge could now be seen down in a great pit; it ran right underneath St Edmund's church. Here were the cellars of the buildings that had been pulled down, filled with rubble. Adam and Donald explored for a time, picking up bits of broken china, sifting through debris, hoping to discover some treasure. But discarded prams and rusty bed-springs seemed to be the only things people left in cellars. They got very dusty, and searching for treasure was too exhausting a job, particularly at the end of a hot August day. They found a huge tunnel with pipes in it, sewer pipes, Donald said. It was like a long cave,

dark, dank and cool. Their voices bounced off the walls in mocking echoes. Water dripped. They did not go far inside; they would need a torch. Anyway, it was tea-time.

'We'll find a way of getting back into the Tudor house,' Adam said.

'How?'

'Meet me there tomorrow. Early. About half past eight.'

'Then what?'

'I'll tell you when I see you.'

They returned to their families. Mrs Webb was annoyed because Adam's clothes were so filthy, but he paid her little attention; he was working out his plan.

There was no objection from Mrs Webb or Mrs Martin about going out so early; crowds of people were expected, so if the children wanted a good view of the move, half past eight did not seem an unreasonable time to be there. But Adam slept restlessly, and was out of bed by seven o'clock. This meant he could enjoy the rare luxury of breakfast alone with his father. Mr Webb was not a very good cook – a boiled egg was all he could manage – but he did everything slowly, and he stopped to talk and answer questions.

'They're pulling the Teignmouth Inn down this morning,' Adam said.

'Yes, I know. I remember it when I was a boy, fetching a jug of beer for my dad, Friday nights. Your mother and I used to go in there when we were courting. And Old Year's Night! We had some grand Old Year's Nights in that pub. Mrs Brealy, the landlady, she was good fun! She had a wig. I remember once she . . . No, I don't think I'd better tell you that one.'

'Why? Is it rude?'

'No.' Adam looked at his father sternly, and his father looked back at him. 'Well, yes, it is a bit.'

They both laughed. These breakfasts with Dad were happy times too.

When he was outside Adam watched the men preparing the foundations next door. This afternoon the Tudor house would be on top of all that wood and concrete. A cat scurried over the site, leaving its footprints in the wet cement. The men shooed it away, but did not bother to remove the footprints. They would harden and be there for ever, Adam thought, even though they would remain invisible underneath the house; a stray cat had left a lasting mark, and the Teignmouth Inn, with all those Old Year's Nights, would soon be only a memory in people's minds! It was strange. He felt he wanted to leave a mark of some sort, too. He didn't know what. He had carved his name on a desk at school, but that was not import-ant, no more than the cat's footprints. The mark must be something more worthwhile than that.

There were quite a few people already waiting by the Tudor house, but the workmen had not yet arrived. Donald was impatient. 'Well, what's happening?' he asked.

'About what?'

'Getting back inside, of course!'

Adam screwed up his eyes and pretended to look thoughtful, but he knew exactly what he was going to do. The house had been winched up about two feet off the ground; it was a simple matter, to start with, of crawling underneath when no-one was looking: then came the hard part, finding the loose floor-boards – there were some, near the back door, that were almost rotten – and pushing them up far enough so that they could wriggle through. He was a bit frightened, however, at the idea of lying under the house. It might fall and crush them to death.

'Just do what I tell you,' he said. 'Do everything I do.' He looked round anxiously; more and more people were appearing every minute. They seemed to be interested chiefly in the great iron wheels that had been attached to the corners of the house; no-one had thought of peering underneath, but the

crowd was too big for him to risk making a dash for it. Fortunately the arrival of the BBC television crew provided a diversion; the sight of men laying out lengths of cable and assembling cameras proved, for a moment, more absorbing, and everyone who was wandering idly round the back of the house moved away to the front.

'Now!' he said, and flinging himself down, he crawled underneath. Donald was only a split second behind him. Adam lay on his back, and levered himself carefully to what he thought was the correct spot. The floor-boards were loose all right, damp, and smelling of autumn trees, but refused to budge. 'Help me!' he cried, and together they pushed. Something gave way slowly, and one of the planks, free at one end, they prised upright. It did not allow sufficient space for them to struggle through, however, so they shoved and kicked at its neighbour.

'I hope it won't make the house wobble,' Donald said.

Adam grunted. 'Push!'

This board wouldn't give at all at its ends; it had been nailed down too firmly. Then it suddenly snapped in the middle, with a tearing noise so loud that they thought for a moment they would be discovered. But no faces peered in at them. They lifted the wood up, and after a little wriggling and heaving they were inside.

'Keep below the window level,' Adam said, 'or we'll be seen.'

'What do we do now?'

'Crawl over to the stairs. We'll creep up to the top floor and we'll stay there. We'll have a marvellous free ride!'

'Isn't it dangerous?'

'I don't think so.'

'What if the house falls over and smashes to pieces? We'll be killed!'

'It won't fall over. The men have done a first class job; my dad said so.' But he was worried, none the less.

I t was quite easy to see out and not be noticed by the crowd in the street. The windows were leaded, and as the glass was old and encrusted with years of dirt, it was difficult for people to observe anything inside the house. Adam and Donald stayed near the centre of the room, and felt they were completely safe from prying eyes. There was one awkward moment when a television camera pointed, it seemed, straight up at them, but they ducked immediately. A few minutes later, when they dared to look again, it was swivelled round in the opposite direction, filming the prepara-

tions for pulling down the Teignmouth Inn. Adam had imagined there would be some sort of crane with a big steel ball which would bash the walls in, but this, apparently, was unnecessary. A thick cable was being tied round the pub, and it looked as if it was going to be attached to a tractor. The Teignmouth Inn was so flimsy that it only needed a piece of wire and a tractor to destroy it! It would be like watching Mr Vickery, the grocer in Fore Street, using the special wire he kept for cutting cheese, only on a much bigger scale of course.

Things were happening now to the Tudor house. The workmen had arrived, and were making a lot of noise as they tightened up nuts and bolts. There was a clonk of metal hitting metal – the iron wheels were being given a last-minute check – and loud hissing noises were coming out of the compressed air machine that operated the pneumatic jacks.

There were no cars now in Edmund Street or Frog Street, and the children could see a policeman on the other side of the church diverting the traffic. The crowd of spectators was enormous; hundreds of them, Adam thought. They stood, several deep on the pavements and in the road itself, and every window at the back of the shops in West Street and Bridge Street was crammed with people. At one end of Frog Street an ice cream stall was doing a brisk trade; at the other a man was busy selling hot dogs. The only empty area was the actual route the Tudor house would take, the straight line of the railway track to the vacant space next to BARRY WEBB. LONDON HAIR FASHIONS. The Tudor house was to be hauled to its new home like an enormous goods wagon.

A sudden violent shudder ran through the timbers; the floor groaned and plaster dropped from the walls. Some of the leaded panes cracked. Adam and Donald nearly fell over, and clutched each other for support. It was as if the house was objecting furiously to the outrage of being moved from the place where it had stood for four centuries, of being ordered off the ground that had rightfully belonged to it since the days of Henry the Eighth and Anne Boleyn. It tilted very slightly.

'It's going to fall!' Adam cried out in fear. 'It's going to collapse!'

'No, it isn't. They're just lowering it on to the rails.'

Donald was right. The shudder stopped, and the house touched the track very gently; there was scarcely a tremor, and the only sound was a faint clink of metal. They started to move, at first so slowly that they were almost unaware of it, except for a jagged screech as the wheels turned. A great cheer went up from the crowd, and St Edmund's tower was not in quite the same place in the window as it had been a few moments before.

The journey was very slow indeed. It took three and a half hours. Inch by inch St Edmund's church crept a little further away; the back of the shops in West Street grew nearer. What a tale they would have to tell! Anyone could say, years later, oh yes, they saw the Tudor house being moved, but he and Donald could say '*We* were *inside!*'

'There's my mum,' said Donald, pointing.

'I can't see her.'

'She's talking to your mum.'

'Oh yes. They must be wondering where we are.'

Mrs Webb and Mrs Martin were nattering nineteen to the dozen, but Mrs Webb kept looking round with a puzzled expression. Obviously she was searching for Adam, and trying to decide what mischief he and Donald were up to now.

'Will you tell them what we're doing?' Adam asked.

'I don't think so. They'd be really mad!' Donald turned and stared out of the window on the other side of the house. 'Look! They're just about to pull down the Teignmouth Inn!'

'Don't go so near the window!'

'Sorry. I forgot for a moment.'

The crowd had been cleared away from the street by the old pub; the television crews, abandoning the Tudor house for a while, focused their attention on the demolition gang. The cable stretched, grew slack, was taut again; the tractor revved up and leaped forward. It stopped, bucking like a frightened horse. The walls of the Teignmouth Inn were stronger, evidently, than people had imagined. The driver tried a second time, and the same thing happened. He switched off the engine, climbed down from his seat, and went back with some other workmen to

inspect the cable, to see if it had had any effect at all. At last they seemed satisfied, and he returned to his tractor. The engine started; the workmen hurriedly left the scene, and this time the cable sliced straight through the building. There was a split second when it appeared that the walls had slipped just fractionally to a strange angle and would not collapse, then, with a tremendous roar like a huge waterfall, they sagged, fell apart, and dropped to the ground in a great pile of bricks, splintered wood and fragments of glass. A huge cloud of yellow-grey dust blew upwards. It hung, motionless for a moment, before it began settling on the rubble and the people watching; then it drifted away over the river towards St Thomas.

The disturbance had little effect on the Tudor house; there were no blast waves such as a bomb would produce. There was a slight hesitation in its movement, and a strange hollow groan as if it was lamenting the death of its younger, less substantial, companion.

'Never seen anything like it!' said Adam, wide-eyed. 'Spec-tac-u-lar!'

'Fan-tas-tic!'

'It makes you wonder, though.'

'What?'

'If it falls to bits that easily, how safe is our house?'

'What, this one?'

'No, home. Where I live.'

'Oh that's daft! Of course it's safe.'

Adam looked towards West Street. It was near enough now for him to make out the things in his mother's kitchen, the potted plant and the canister of Vim on the window-sill, a saucepan on the stove. 'I'm hungry,' he announced.

'I've brought some food,' Donald said. 'Marmite sandwiches, two tomatoes, two apples and some biscuits.'

'That's great! You think of everything.'

'I thought we might be in here for a long time. So I asked Mum for something to eat; said we were going on a picnic.'

'I wonder if anybody ever starved to death in here?'

'Shouldn't think so.' Donald's mouth was full of biscuit.

'A prisoner who died of hunger.' It turned into a game. The house was a mobile siege engine in the Middle Ages; Adam had been captured by Perkin Warbeck's men, and if he didn't tell where the secret underground passages into the city were, he would be sentenced to death by starvation. Or hanged from St Edmund's tower as a reprisal against the citizens. They had just decided on the latter when they were brought back to reality by changes in the noise and movement underneath them. The house had arrived. It was being winched up off the metal track. Once again it objected by tilting slightly and shuddering in all its timbers. Then silence.

'What's happening?' Donald asked.

Adam crept as near the window as he dared. 'I think the men are knocking off for dinner. Yes, they are. They're going towards the quay. To the *Bishop Blaize*, I expect.'

'What do we do? How do we get out?'

'Simple. Simpler than I'd thought. They haven't lowered it on to its new foundations yet, so we can go the same way as we came in. I was afraid we'd have to climb out of one of the windows or something.'

They went downstairs to where the broken floorboards were. They could easily have been spotted by people outside, but now that the house had arrived, the spectators were losing interest and beginning to leave. The gap between the floor and the new concrete was about the same size as the one they had crawled through earlier. Down in the hole

Adam could see the cat's footprints, now firm and dry, fixed for ever. They squeezed themselves into the little space and edged out into the sunlight. Once again they were lucky. No-one saw them.

They brushed the dust and grime off their clothes. 'See you later,' Adam said.

'After tea. I have to go shopping with Mum this afternoon.'

Where had he been all morning, Mrs Webb wanted to know, and why was he so dirty *twice* in two days? *And* it was long past dinner-time.

'I was watching the house being moved,' he answered, quite truthfully.

'Well, I didn't see you,' she said. 'I looked all over the place.'

'I was there all right. I saw you.'

She gave him a very peculiar look, then turned away to take his meal out of the oven. He caught his father's eye: Dad seemed to know something. Adam frowned. Dad continued to stare, but it was an expression that might well be saying, I won't mention a word about it.

The local news on the television that night showed the Teignmouth Inn disintegrating and the Tudor house travelling on the various stages of its triumphant journey from Frog Street to West Street. Adam watched, fascinated; it presented views of the whole operation that he had missed. A house on wheels did look remarkably like some ancient kind of siege engine, he thought. Then the newscaster's words made him gasp. 'Rumours have been circulating all day that Exeter's Tudor house may be haunted. Several people in the crowd claim to have seen the faces of two boys behind

a window on the top storey. An elderly woman said they were wearing clothes of the Elizabethan period. Other witnesses simply remarked on the presence of the faces, and one man, Mr Warren of Budleigh Salterton, thought that they had no bodies. Speculation is rife that two children may have met a violent death in the house. Its early history is not known for certain, but a search is to be made tomorrow in the City Record Office for any documents that might solve the mystery. Something that resembles the faces can be seen on our film now, but experts think it is probably a trick of the light.'

Adam felt himself blush scarlet. There he was, in the middle of the window, Donald beside him. The picture lasted for about ten seconds, then the whole item ended. The newscaster was talking about the cricket match at Taunton between Somerset and

Hampshire. Adam slowly looked up at his father.

Mr Webb took his pipe out of his mouth. 'What do you make of that?' he asked.

'I . . . don't know.'

'Don't you?' Adam said nothing. 'I think you do, young man. And I also think it was very dangerous and very silly. To be inside that house when it was being moved! If it had collapsed you would both have been killed!'

'Yes . . . I . . . er . . . suppose so.'

'You ought to have more sense.' He picked up the newspaper and started to read.

'Dad.'

'Yes?'

'I'm sorry.'

'Nothing did happen, but that's not the point. Don't you ever do anything like that again!' Mr Webb returned to the paper, and Adam concentrated on the television. After a few moments, a rather peculiar noise made him look at his father. Dad's whole body was shaking with laughter.

'Haunted!' he said at last, and wiped his eyes. 'My son is a decapitated Elizabethan ghost! Whatever will they think of next?'

Adam relaxed. He had been afraid Dad would be severe; doing dangerous things usually made him very angry. 'What's decapitated?' he asked.

'Having your head cut off. Don't you know that, child? Oh dear, oh dear, oh dear! Adam, the ghost of the Tudor house!'

'You won't tell anyone, Dad? Please!'

'No, no, certainly not. I'd hate to spoil people's pleasure! I won't even tell your mother. On second thoughts *especially* not your mother. She wouldn't see the funny side of it at all!' He laughed again. 'People will believe anything! The simplest explanation, two kids up to no good, is the last thing they'll think of!'

Later that evening Adam and Donald were standing outside the Tudor house. It was growing dark, and the house cast a long black shadow on the walls of St Mary Steps church on the opposite side of the street. It was a shadow that had never appeared before, because where the house was had always been an empty open space.

'It doesn't look too bad there,' Adam said. 'Quite solid.' It had been lowered on to its foundations during the afternoon, and some of the wood the workmen had bolted on to it had been removed. 'I suppose we'll get used to it, in time.'

They did get used to it, of course, but they never played in the Tudor house again. Another gang of workmen arrived next day to plaster and paint, repair floorboards, put in electrical wiring and plumbing, and they were less friendly than the men who had brought the house from Frog Street. As soon as they were finished, Mr Milton, the antique dealer, moved in, and the house was filled with furniture, brass and silver ornaments, and all kinds of nick-nacks. Someone came to paint the sign over the door, ALBERT MILTON: TUDOR ANTIQUES, in gold lettering. And if anybody thought they were going to pick up a real Tudor antique in there, Mr Webb remarked, they were in for a disappointment; most of the stuff was junk.

Mr Milton, however, turned out to be a pleasant sort of neighbour, and Mrs Webb stopped worrying that all antique dealers were crooks. 'The exception proves the rule,' she said.

The only part of the story that was not forgotten quickly was the belief that the Tudor house was haunted. Many people reported sightings of the children, late at

night peering out of the windows, and though the search in the City Record Office did not reveal anything about a murder having taken place there in Tudor times, a team of professional ghost-hunters was called in. They

77

carried out all sorts of elaborate tests, but found nothing. This seemed to satisfy everyone's curiosity, and, after a while, the story ceased to be of interest. Adam and Donald kept very quiet about it, but Mr Webb continued to be highly amused. 'People will believe anything,' he repeated.

THE GHOST AT NO. 13
Gyles Brandreth

Hamlet Brown's sister, Susan, is just too perfect. Everything she does is praised and Hamlet is in despair – until a ghost comes to stay for a holiday and helps him to find an exciting idea for his school project!

RADIO DETECTIVE
John Escott

A piece of amazing deduction by the Roundhay Radio Detective when Donald, the radio's young presenter, solves a mystery but finds out more than anyone expects.

RAGDOLLY ANNA'S CIRCUS
Jean Kenward

Made only from a morsel of this and a tatter of that, Ragdolly Anna is a very special doll and the six stories in this book are all about her adventures.

SEE YOU AT THE MATCH
Margaret Joy

Six delightful stories about football. Whether spectator, player, winner or loser these short, easy stories for young readers are a must for all football fans.